THE PETER RABBIT CLUB

PUFFIN

Map of my woods

This is a map of the woods where I live. You can see who else lives here too. It's in my dad's journal which I always have with me.

ROCKY ISLAND

Old Brown is very bad tempered. We stay away from him.

OLD BROWN'S ISLAND

MR JEREMY FISHER'S POND

SQUIRREL NUTKIN'S WOOD

MRS TIGGY-WINKLE'S LAUNDRY

Tommy Brock is a badger who loves worms, but hates rabbits!

This is **Mr Tod**. Foxes eat rabbits. Need I say more?

JEMIMA PUDDLE-DUCK'S HILLTOP FARM

MR McGREGOR'S GARDEN

MR TOD & TOMMY BROCK'S WOOD

MY BURROW

My friend, **Lily Bobtail**. Whatever the problem, she's got the answer.

DR & MRS BOBTAIL'S BURROW (LILY'S HOME)

TUNNEL NETWORK

MR BOUNCER'S BURROW (BENJAMIN'S HOME)

RAVINE

DEEP DARK WOODS

DANDELION FIELD

Benjamin Bunny is my cousin. Whatever I do, he's right behind me – usually hiding!

One sunny morning, Peter, Lily and Benjamin were at their secret treehouse wondering what to do that day.

"Let's start a club!" announced Peter. "The Brave Adventurers Club!"

"We'll have AMAZING adventures!" cried Lily.

"Can we call it the Tummy Club?" asked Benjamin. "I like snack adventures!"

Little did the friends know
that nearby three of the worst
villains in the woods were
hatching a terrible plot.

"Let's join together and get those rabbits once and
for all!" said Mr Tod. "I want rabbit stew for dinner!"

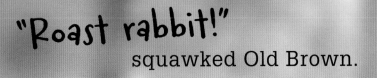

"Roast rabbit!"
squawked Old Brown.

"Rabbit on toast,"
agreed Tommy Brock.
"Though rabbits aren't as tasty as worms."

Meanwhile, the unsuspecting bunnies were having a snack adventure in Mr McGregor's garden.

"We're the Cucumber Chompers Club,"
said Benjamin.

"We're the Lettuce Lovers,"
giggled Lily, nibbling a leaf.

"Uh-oh, someone's coming," whispered Peter.

"Radish Raiders,
let's hop to it!"

But as the friends ran
towards the garden gate . . .

"Leaving so soon?" hissed Mr Tod, licking his lips. "But it's nearly time for lunch!"

"Run!" cried Peter, spotting one of his dad's emergency escape tunnels.

But as the rabbits DIVED for the entrance . . .

"This tunnel's closed!"

said Tommy Brock, jumping in the way.

Just then, Peter spotted a long wooden
plank leaning against the garden wall.

"Follow me!"
he called to Benjamin and Lily.

The rabbits raced
up the ramp . . .

. . . just as Old Brown swooped down, sending them tumbling back to the ground.

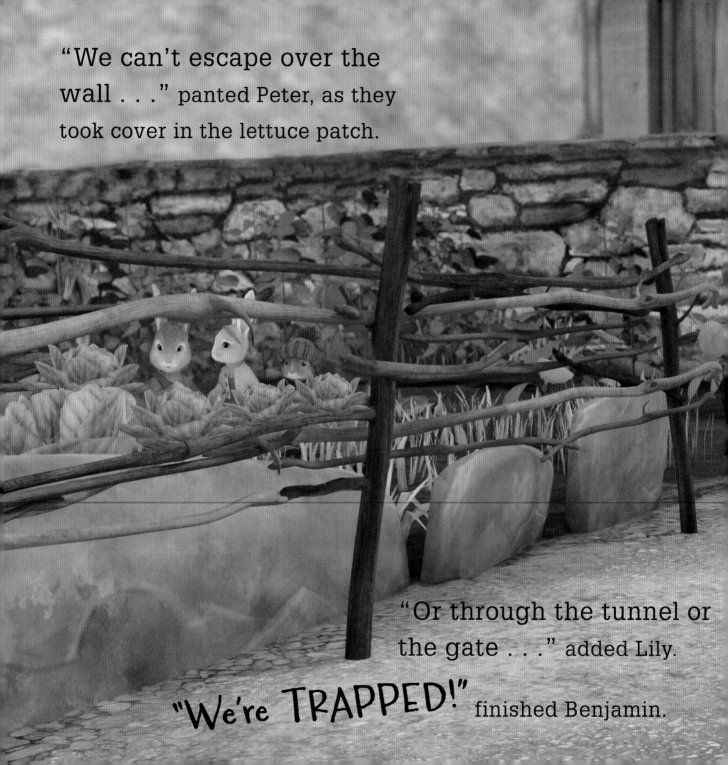

"We can't escape over the wall . . ." panted Peter, as they took cover in the lettuce patch.

"Or through the tunnel or the gate . . ." added Lily.

"We're TRAPPED!" finished Benjamin.

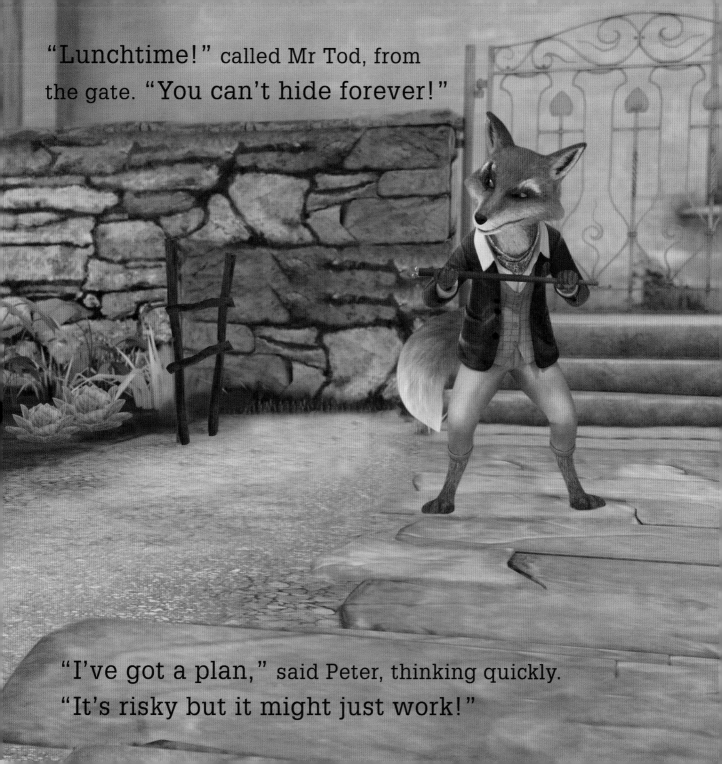

"Lunchtime!" called Mr Tod, from the gate. "You can't hide forever!"

"I've got a plan," said Peter, thinking quickly. "It's risky but it might just work!"

Peter hopped over to where
Tommy Brock was still guarding
the tunnel entrance.

"Tommy Brock!"
called Peter, waving a
wiggling worm. "How
about a juicy snack
while you're waiting?"

"Oi, give it here!"
shouted the hungry badger.

"Come and get it!"
Peter called, turning
and racing away.

"STOP!"
yelled Mr Tod, charging after
Peter and Tommy Brock.

"We're supposed to
share those rabbits!"

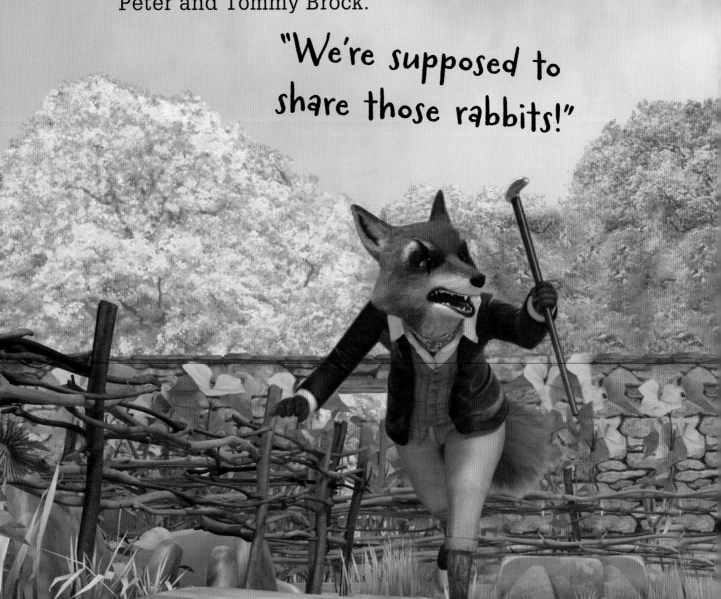

"Hey, save some rabbit for me!" squawked Old Brown, joining the chase.

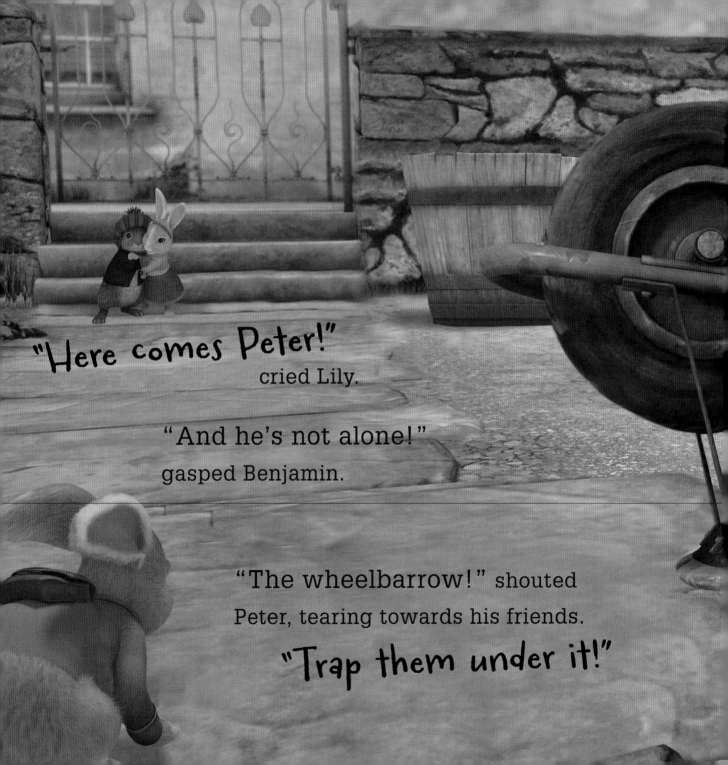

"Here comes Peter!"
cried Lily.

"And he's not alone!"
gasped Benjamin.

"The wheelbarrow!" shouted
Peter, tearing towards his friends.
"Trap them under it!"

Quickly, Lily leaped into action. She grabbed some sturdy string from her Just-in-Case Pocket and looped it around the stick propping up Mr McGregor's rusty old wheelbarrow.

Peter raced under
the barrow and out
the other side.

The villains dived after him . . .

. . . just as Lily and Benjamin gave the string a hard tug, bringing the wheelbarrow down on top of Mr Tod and his treacherous team – **CRASH!**

"Hey, let us out!"

"Tail feathers!"

"I'll get you next time, PETER RABBIT!"

The bunnies made their escape.

Back at the secret treehouse, the friends tucked into some yummy radishes Peter had stashed in his satchel.

"Great teamwork, Awesome Adventurers Club!" said Peter.

"Peter," said Lily, "the club was your idea. So let's just call ourselves . . .

The Peter Rabbit Club!"

OUR SECRET CLUBHOUSE

Our treetop hideout is the perfect place to escape from Mr Tod and his gang. It's also a brilliant base for planning adventures!

Nature nook

Escape hatch

Pull weight to open trapdoor onto high-speed escape chute

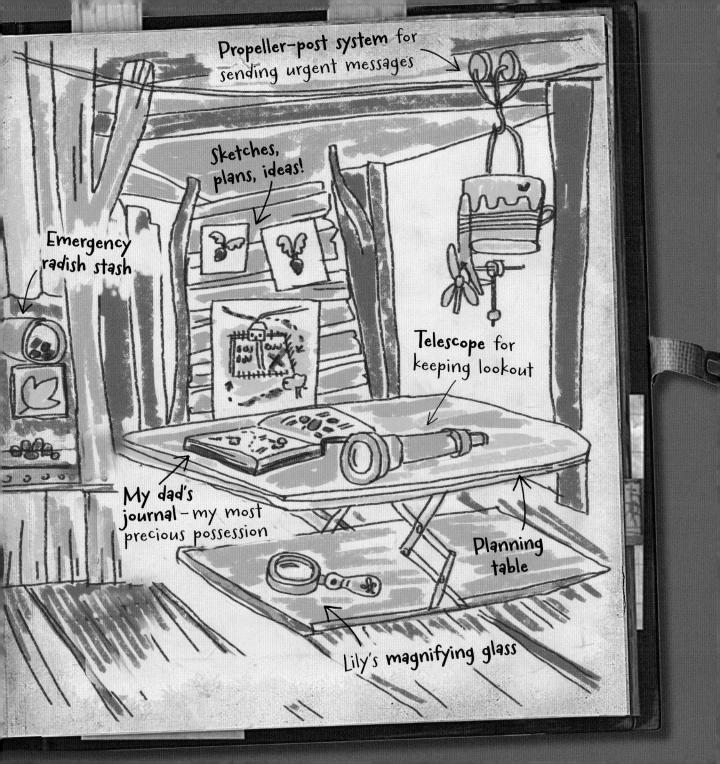

Build your own
SECRET CLUBHOUSE

Peter, Lily and Benjamin's clubhouse in sky-high Squirrel Camp is built from all kinds of bits and bobs.

You can make your own secret clubhouse – it doesn't have to be in a tree!

AT HOME

Hang a sheet between two chairs to make a cosy hideaway. Cushions make sturdy walls.

OUTSIDE

Look out for secret spots in your garden or park. Inside big bushes or under low trees are good places to try.

CONGRATULATIONS!
THE PETER RABBIT CLUB
MEMBER'S CERTIFICATE

Awarded to

Age

Peter Rabbit

CLUB LEADER

Welcome to our club!

Go to www.peterrabbitclub.com for more ideas for fun things to do and Peter Rabbit Club badges to collect!